The Lesson

A Story of Hope and Redemption

Stories for Grandma Series

Jimmy Hickey

The Lesson: A Story of Hope and Redemption
ISBN: Softcover 978-1-955581-76-9
Copyright © 2022 by Jimmy Hickey

Parson's Porch Books is an imprint of Parson's Porch & Company (PP&C) in Cleveland, Tennessee. PP&C is an innovative organization which raises money by publishing books of noted authors, representing all genres. Its face and voice is **David Russell Tullock** (dtullock@parsonsporch.com).

Parson's Porch & Company *turns books into bread & milk* by sharing its profits with the poor.

www.parsonsporch.com

The Lesson

Little… Or Much?

In squelched frustration, Pastor Raymond Miller made his weekly appeal to his meager Sunday morning flock on the importance of Sunday night prayer meetings.

"It's the time of the week when we come together as the body of Christ to seek God on behalf of the members as well as for the direction our church should be heading. Please make an effort to be here tonight."

And like every other week, only about a dozen showed up.

"Not even representing 10 percent of the congregation," calculated Pastor Miller to his head usher Earl Barclay. Brother Barclay was a wiry old black man with fuzzy grey hair and watery grey eyes. But his spirit was vibrant, and he seemed to have the energy of a man half his age. Since his life companion of a wife died 15 years ago, he would be in church every time the door opened. From services to prayer meetings to appointments with the building inspector, you'd always find Brother Barclay in church. And if you asked him why, he would simply quote the apostle Peter, "Lord, to whom shall we go? You have the words of eternal life."

"I reckon we got two-hunnerd folks come to this chu-ch. We oughta have two-hunnerd folks prayin'," reasoned Brother Barclay.

"That's what I figure," Pastor Miller agreed. "But it's like this every week. We need to stir up these folks to good works as the Bible says. Any ideas?"

"Ah, now, now, Pastuh. You talkin' 'bout stirrin' the pot. They's either gonna unite togethuh, else they's gonna run scared!"

"Well, I want to make sure whatever we do, it's going to bring everybody together," Pastor Miller snapped his fingers. "I have an idea. Let's do a dish-to-pass dinner after next Sunday's service."

The old man just laughed at his pastor. "Yes, suh! That'll really bring 'em togethuh! Chu-ch folks sho' loves to eat! Yes, suh!"

So, word got out quickly about dinner after next Sunday's service and everyone brought food to share. Pastor Miller delivered his sermon on needing to do more things together as a family. He used scriptures to teach that every person who names the name of the Lord Jesus has their particular function as a member of Christ's body; as a part of Christ's church. And EVERYONE is needed to do their part.

It seemed to Pastor Miller that the "Amen's" were heartier this week and he hoped this was just the shove people needed to get more involved. By the time prayer service began at seven o'clock, there were 50 people waiting to pray! "Now that's more like it!" he expressed to Brother Barclay.

"Yes, suh! You stirred somethin' up alright."

By the following Sunday, Pastor Miller had a few more ideas up his sleeve, but decided he'd better start off slow… one at a time for now. "Next Sunday, let's have another dish-to-pass dinner, what do you think?"

He got a few hearty "Amen's."

"What do you say to dish-to-pass dinners every other week?"

A few more hearty "Amen's."

Pastor Miller was beaming at this point. "Alright, so we are on for every other week. Sister Gilder, will you mark your calendar in order to announce the reminders in our bulletin?" The part-time secretary affirmed.

Changing the subject, the pastor decided to introduce Plan A. "This coming Friday night, I want us to meet here as a church family. And together we are going to go out on the streets and evangelize. This means we must go to where the people are, so we'll probably end up near some pretty shady places. That's why we need everyone's participation.

Strength in numbers, that sort of thing." Then he reminded them of prayer service that night and how this effort will be one of the focuses of their petitions.

That evening, just under 30 congregates gathered for prayer. Pastor Miller decided this was still better than the dozen or so they were getting before. Brother Barclay agreed.

The designated Friday night arrived, and Brother Barclay appeared in a worn-out old jacket and walking shoes. Pastor Miller smiled when he saw him.

"I can always count on you, old faithful friend."

"I cain't help it, Pastuh. Jesus is always faithful to me. I gots to retu-n the favor!"

"I hope I never forget that," reflected Pastor Miller.

Seven p.m. came and went. The pastor and his usher were still the only two evangelists at the church. Finally, at ten minutes after, a car pulled in. It was the Seavers; a young couple who had only been coming to the church for about four months. They had a well-behaved one-year old daughter named Trudy. Gary and Tonya stepped out of their car.

"Sorry we're late. We had to pick up the babysitter and take her back to our place so she could watch Trudy for the night," explained Tonya.

"Where is everybody?" worried Gary, "Are we still going out?"

"Yes, we're still going out," encouraged Pastor Miller who was himself not feeling very encouraged. "It looks like we're it, though."

"I don't understand," Gary expressed. "Shouldn't there be more people here? What happened to 'strength in numbers'?"

Pastor Miller settled him. "We just have to rethink our strategy. It seems to me that with only four of us, we'll concentrate on a less immoral area. Neutral ground if you know what I mean."

"You mean like where regular people are?" asked Tonya.

"Well, since we's reg'lar people, that seems to make the most sense!" smiled Brother Barclay.

Pastor Miller smiled, too. "So, the perfect spot is where a lot of people go, at all kinds of hours, and we see all classes or characters."

They all thought for a minute. Gary burst the silence. "The truck stop!" he practically yelled.

The pastor nodded his head, "The truck stop."

"I'll drive!" Gary burst again with nervous excitement.

Mama's 24-hour Truck Stop was a permanent fixture right off the highway – "Easy off, Easy on." It was the most popular place to do business… and not all of it legitimate. Situated between two major vendor cities, the establishment attracted almost everyone in the state to its little borough.

It had always been a gas station as far back as anyone could remember, until Mama took it over in 1983. After that, Mama herself became a permanent fixture behind the cigarette counter. No matter what time of day you came in, it seemed you would always find her sitting in the beat up, leather, swivel, office chair – all 300 pounds of her. She wore a greasy sleeveless top and flip flops. There was a Marlboro cigarette hanging out of her mouth… sometimes it was lit. But years of smoking had given her that raspy voice which makes you want to clear your throat for her. Probably the only feminine thing about her was the jumbo cup of Diet Coke she constantly sipped from a straw.

Mama never participated in illegal activity. And while she knew it was taking place on her property, she never was aware of the particulars. This was the same answer she gave to the police, too, whenever they were dispatched on suspicion. They called her "Mama" like everyone else, because frankly, no one knew her real name.

Armed with tracts and pocket Bibles, the vibrant little street team made way to their respective posts. Pastor Miller suggested they pair off; the Seavers would hit the dining room while he and Brother Barclay would talk to truckers and whomever else lingered outside.

The Seavers immediately found a young couple like themselves with a young child who were just passing through on the way to the big Metropolis. They sat with the couple to talk with and to minister to them.

Pastor Miller and Barclay talked with truckers and people filling up their vehicles with gas. Not getting much response from the evangelism angle, the brothers tried something different. They told the people they were from the local church and taking prayer requests. This opened the door, and many had a request. Some even stood with the pastor and usher right in the parking lot to pray.

Throughout the evening, Pastor Miller saw movement in the shadows. He would hear a rap on a truck door, which would open and close. Then a little while later he would see a head peer out from around a truck. As soon as he glanced over, the face would disappear into the shadows… which would be followed by a rap on a truck door.

After three hours or so of seeing this person then not seeing them, Pastor Miller brought it to Brother Barclay's attention. "I keep seeing someone in the shadows over there. I think they're watching us."

"Whaddya wanna do, Pastuh?"

"Pray, brother. Pray that God will entice them out into the open so we can minister to their needs."

Well, it worked… the brother prayed, and God drew the figure out into the light. And Pastor Miller was waiting. But he wasn't expecting what he saw. Being a single man, once in a while the devil had used this to entice the man of God. God had been faithful to provide a way of escape for this pastor on every occasion. And tonight would be no different. However, when the scantily clad woman with all the important parts hanging out emerged from the shadows, Pastor Miller found it very difficult to keep his eyes from scoping out the situation.

Fortunately the woman, an obvious prostitute, saw this but did not hold it against him. She approached the men rather boldly and asked in deep southern drawl what they were doing there. "Y'all bein' here is ruinin' my tricks tonight."

Brother Barclay used the line they'd been reciting all night. "We're here from the chu-ch and we're takin' prayer requests."

She became curious, "Y'all are just prayin'?"

"What's your name, ma'am?" asked Pastor Miller, finally fortified by seeing her desperate need for Jesus.

"Why do you want to know my name? Y'all want some of this?" She shifted her stance as though to display her merchandise.

Pastor Miller was not swayed, however. "No, ma'am. But I think *you* want some of this."

Immediately her countenance changed, and she attempted to cover herself up, which didn't work.

Pastor Miller removed his jacket and offered it to the woman. She humbly accepted with a half-smile, "Thanks."

"Would you like to go inside for a cup of coffee?" "That'd be nice," she drawled.

When they entered the diner Mama hollered, "Vixie, I told you, you can't solicit in here!"

Vixie spat back, "I ain't, Mama! The Reverend (she emphasized) wants to buy me a cup of coffee."

"You shameless bitch! You's taking in reverends now?" cigarette ash flipping all over herself.

Vixie dropped her head like a scolded puppy. But Pastor Miller was quick with a rebuttal. "If you'd give us a chance, Mama, you'd see we're the ones trying to do the 'taking in'." Mama cough-laughed, "Yer wastin' yer time with that one. She's a lost cause." The two men just led the woman to a corner table for some semblance of privacy.

Pastor Miller spoke. Brother Barclay prayed under his breath. He figured he'd best let the pastor handle this one. "There are no lost causes, Vixie."

She slumped her shoulders. "My real name's Angela."

"Pleased to meet you, Angela. I'm Pas... uh, Raymond Miller. This is my friend Barclay." She cautiously shook their hands, meeting Barclay's eyes for an extended moment.

"So, y'all been takin' prayers?" she began. "That's right," pastor answered.

"You think it'd work for me?"

"I *know* when a person calls on God and sincerely wants God to intervene in their life, then He will answer."

Angela sat up as straight as she could and tried to sound professional... or was it distant... maybe she was just numb. "I works really hard. And I get paid *really* good, if you know what I mean."

Pastor Miller kept his eyes on her with genuine interest. But he didn't feel a response was appropriate at this point. He was right.

She continued, "Anyway, I know this ain't no way for a girl to make a living. 'Specially since it won't last forever."

A waitress brought their coffees and all the fixin's. She made no attempt at eye contact, nor did she speak.

Angela sipped the bitter black liquid and waited while it warmed her insides. The men waited, sipping from their cups.

Finally she just gushed it all out as though she'd been holding her breath and was starving for oxygen. "Ok, here's the thing. I have a four-year old boy who is the love of my life. I don't know who the father is, obviously. Call it an occupational hazard. I take care of him during the day, then take him to my mother's to spend the night while I work. She thinks I'm a waitress here. She doesn't get out much, ya know?

"Anyway, I know what I'm doing is… uh… well, let's call it bad. I know it's bad and it's not the way I was raised. But it's all I know how to do. And considering the package I have to work with, I'm *really* good at it."

She waited, but Pastor Miller outlasted her figuring there was more. "Well? Can you make a prayer outta that?" she asked.

Pastor Miller decided to ask some clarifiers first. "Is your mother married?"

"She is, but Daddy left when I was a little girl. I haven't seen him since."

"So, you grew up without your father and your son is potentially following the same path."

"It looks that way."

"You also said your occupation was all you know how to do. Are you sure you never tried anything else?"

"When I was in school, I got passed around from boy to boy. At one point I realized, 'Hey, y'all are just usin' me, so I might as well get paid for it.' Didn't last long, though. The school heard about it and kicked me out."

"You never went back?"

"Never went back."

Pastor Miller's heart was breaking. He didn't know what he could do for the woman. But he knew Someone who could. Was there a chance this poor destitute woman would forsake the life she's chosen for what Jesus had to offer?

Suddenly, an idea struck him. He pulled a little Bible from his pocket and turned to John 8.

"Have you ever heard about Jesus?"

Angela p'shawed, "Who hasn't?"

Pastor Miller disregarded this and began to read… from verse 2:

...but early the next morning Jesus was back again at the Temple. A crowd soon gathered, and he sat down and taught them. 3 As he was speaking, the teachers of religious law and the Pharisees brought a woman who had been caught in the act of adultery. They put her in front of the crowd.

4   "Teacher," they said to Jesus, "this woman was caught in the act of adultery...

His voice caught in his throat and tears threatened to flood from his eyes. Angela watched enrapt as Pastor Miller struggled to finish the account:

5   The law of Moses says to stone her. What do you say?"

6   They were trying to trap him into saying something they could use against him, but Jesus stooped down and wrote in the dust with his finger. 7 They kept demanding an answer, so he stood up again and said, "All right, but let the one who has never sinned throw the first stone!" 8 Then he stooped down again and wrote in the dust.

9 When the accusers heard this, they slipped away one by one, beginning with the oldest, until only Jesus was left in the middle of the crowd with the woman. 10 Then Jesus stood up again and said to the woman, "Where are your accusers? Didn't even one of them condemn you?" 11 "No, Lord," she said.

And Jesus said, "Neither do I. Go and sin no more."

He put the Bible down gently and dried his eyes with a napkin. "I'm sorry, Angela. That has never happened to me before. And I must've read it a couple dozen times."

Finally able to blink and close her gaping mouth, in a voice barely audible she asked, "Well?… did she?"

Pastor smiled, the tears starting up again, "What would *you* do?"

It was Angela's turn to cry. "Are you sayin' He don't condemn me for what I done?"

"Listen Angela, Jesus is the only person who ever lived that has the right to condemn you. And

NO… He… Does… Not!"

Angela cried, reached out and grabbed Pastor Miller's hands who cried right along with her.

Brother Barclay covered his eyes with his hands and wept silently to himself.

They remained speechless for a long time. Finally, she gathered her strength up and asked, "Where do we go from here?" And that was it. Like she had just now decided to "go and sin no more" and follow Jesus. And she wanted to know what was supposed to happen next. If He was leading her out of that lifestyle, where was He going to take her?

"How about I take you home," suggested Pastor Miller.

Angela refused, "I don't think I should be alone right now."

"Then stay at your Mom's place a couple days while we figure this thing out together." He eased out of his chair and asked Brother Barclay to borrow the keys to the Seavers' car. "I'll come by so we can talk."

"I'd like that," she smiled as she stood up. They walked out to the little hatchback. Pastor Miller opened the door for her, then went to the driver's side. Barclay came out with the keys. "Ride with me please, Brother, and continue to pray."

Barclay nodded and hopped in the backseat.

As they were going, Pastor Miller noticed Angela appeared a little uncomfortable. "Anything wrong?" he asked.

"You have a kid, too? Are you married?"

"Huh?" He looked at her and spotted the baby carrier in the backseat. "Oh." This caused him to laugh. "This car belongs to the Seavers in my parish. They have a one-year-old."

Angela relaxed a little. "So… you're not married?"

"No, I'm single."

"So, I don't have to worry about what a wife thinks of you driving around town with a prostitute?"

Brother Barclay spoke for the first time from the back. "Ex-prostitute." Pastor Miller and Angela exchanged smiles.

When they pulled up in front of her mother's house, Pastor Miller put the car in park. He got out and ran around to open the door for Angela. They walked to the front door. "You'll call me, then?"

Pastor Miller shook his head, "Nuh-uh. I'm coming by. Stay here."

"Ok, what are we going to talk about?"

"Well, first thing we have to do is get you established in a family. You should come to church on Sun…"

"Oh, no," she interrupted. "I don't think I'm ready for that, yet."

"Ok, well we'll talk. Goodnight, Angela." "Goodnight, Raymond."

And with that, he took off to go pick up the Seavers and call it a night.

Sunday morning found Pastor Miller in the pulpit and guess what scripture text he used for his sermon? That's right! John 8. He spoke on Jesus not condemning us when He could have. Also, there were no lost causes. He didn't use personal examples from Friday night but called the Seavers up to testify.

At the dish-to-pass, everyone was just about to sit down to eat when a stranger walked in. She was dressed in her Sunday best, which wasn't much of a Sunday outfit. In fact, it hardly covered much at all. And her makeup was painted on pretty thick. She was stepping gently in her high heels and carrying a large casserole dish.

Some of the ladies saw Angela and started whispering to themselves. Unconsciously, or maybe consciously, they appeared to put distance between themselves and her. Being somewhat used to cold shoulder treatment, she approached one woman cradling her toddler and asked the obvious, "Is this the covered dish supper?"

The woman turned as if to shield her child from the stranger, "Yes."

Angela asked, "Can you show me where to put this?"

The mother made room on the table without making eye contact while conversations shifted from whispers to nervous chatter. You could even hear some wives scolding their husbands who were forced to look into their laps.

Brother Barclay approached Angela. "Hello, my deah. So good of you to come."

Angela smiled at the familiar face. She gave him an embrace that could only be described as 'professional courtesy.' "Barclay, it's good to see a friendly face," she commented aloud.

Barclay smiled, "Jus give 'em a chance to warm up."

"Mm-hmm, where's the Reverend?"

Pointing to the other end of the room, he directed, "Sittin' down yonder at the head of the table."

With all eyes on her, the room grew quiet as Angela made her way to Pastor Miller. The closer she got, the less composed she felt. There were whispers all around and the tough exterior she walked in with shattered by the time she made it to his chair. She knelt on the floor, threw herself into his bosom and sobbed uncontrollably.

Pastor Miller saw her coming but was not expecting this display. He had invited her yesterday when they talked about what direction to take her life. They agreed to just go one day at a time for now. But he did talk her into coming to dinner to meet his 'family.' "You have to cook something, though," he had instructed.

He embraced her and stroked her hair. He melted his chin down near her ear, so he could whisper softly to her. There were comments and complaints all around. People were wondering what their beloved pastor had gotten himself into. He continued whispering encouragements to Angela until someone spoke up. "Pastor Miller, do you even know who this woman is?"

Pastor Miller looked at all the faces which had gathered around to gawk. He spotted others who had fled to the kitchen to wash dishes or who 'just remembered the ketchup.' In a low voice he admitted, "Of course I know who she is. I invited her." To Angela he asked, "Are you ready?"

She finally looked up at him. Her makeup was all smeared. He gave her his handkerchief and helped her to her feet. While she wiped her face, he spoke. "Brothers and Sisters, this is Angela. We met the other night at the truck stop."

Whispers again, all around… recognition. Someone emboldened uttered, "Lot lizard."

Pastor Miller ignored them. He held Angela's hand while he spoke. "I invited her to dinner today because I wanted her to meet my family. And quite frankly I'm surprised at you. I'm surprised at you all.

"I wanted so much to be able to introduce her to you as the newest member of the family of God. Sure she doesn't look like you, talk like you, or even act like you. But that by no means excludes her. Jesus brought her a long way, but she still has a long way to go. For that matter, we all do." Some of the members nodded their heads in agreement.

Pastor Miller didn't let up. "I'm reminded of the account in scripture where Jesus was invited to eat at the religious leader's house and the sinful woman crashed the party."

He felt Angela tense up at the end of his arm. He held her even tighter, his voice grew stronger. "Simon, the owner of the house, was ready to condemn the woman just for showing up at his home.

"But Jesus offered a parable instead. He said, 'Two men borrowed money from their master; one $50, the other $500. Neither of them could pay the debt so the master canceled both. Now which man do you suppose loved the master most?'"

He waited for a reply. "Barclay?" he assigned.

Brother Barclay quoted it word for word, "I suppose the one whom he forgave more."

Pastor Miller continued, "Jesus completed the parable by declaring, 'This woman whose sins are many has been forgiven. Therefore she loved much. But to whom little is forgiven, the same loves little."

All around the room there were still gawkers, but some bowed their heads because they understood where the pastor was going.

Pastor Miller concluded, "Angela came here today for one reason only… and not because I invited her. Well, that's part of the reason. Anyway, she's here because she has got a lot of love in her heart to share! Couldn't that mean it is because she has been forgiven much!?! And if this congregation hasn't greeted her as an equal, hasn't shown any love or only a little love, could it be that we are in danger of only being forgiven of little!?!"

And with that, Pastor Miller's energy was spent. He embraced Angela and wept. She held him back and held him up. She wept into his shoulder.

When Pastor Miller opened his eyes, they were surrounded. There wasn't a dry eye in the whole dining room. EVERYONE wanted to meet or embrace their new Sister in Christ. She smiled and greeted and embraced them back.

At the end of the line came Brother Barclay. He embraced them both. "Well, you done it Pastuh!"

"Did what, Barclay?"

"You stirred 'em up to unite togethuh. Jus' look at 'em!"

At last, Pastor Miller instructed everyone to sit down and eat, "now that the food is probably cold." They all laughed. Barclay ushered a chair next to his pastor for Angela. She sat and the pastor started to push the chair in for her. He asked, "Did you cook something?"

"No," she confessed.

"No!?!" he stopped pushing.

"I brought somethin', but I didn't cook it." He smiled and finished his gentlemanly deed.

"Mom made it and told me to lie and tell you I cooked it. She insisted I had to impress 'that wonderful preacher man,' she said."

"Wonderful preacher man?"

Angela beamed, "That's what she said. She wants you to think I can cook."

"What is it?"

"Some chicken thing."

Pastor Miller laughed. "So why's your mom insisting you impress me?"

Angela winked, "I'm not sure, but I think she's making plans for me."

"Plans, huh? Well, I guess it's good we're taking this one day at a time."

She grinned and bowed her head, "Yeah, one day at a time."

The Reflection

It had only been six months.

Well… it had been six very *long* months according to Angela Chiccone. Despite what you may think, it's not easy for an ex-prostitute to find work when she has no other skills. Pastor Raymond Miller had been attempting to help the best he could, trying to connect her with organizations or calling in favors. But so far, nothing solid had manifested.

She thought he was sweet for all his trouble. They knew the road would be rocky when they began this venture together ALL those months ago. She figured for sure he would eventually redirect his efforts to someone more worthy… like someone in his congregation. She left his church – or rather, never really started going in the first place. She didn't want Ray to be her pastor. He did not introduce himself that way in the beginning. So she wanted to simply keep him as a friend. (Besides, "Pastor Miller" just sounded too… weird).

And it worked out well. He came over every Tuesday night and studied the Bible with Angela and her mom, Ruby. (Without her steady "income," Angela lost her apartment and so moved back in with Mom). They had gone through the gospel of John. When they got to the same account in chapter 8 which brought them together in the first place, they both broke down and cried… all over again. Ruby asked for an explanation.

Ray mediated while Angela confessed the lifestyle she had been living to her mother. He also facilitated the forgiveness and reconciliation which took place two weeks later. Ruby had taken the news very hard and almost kicked Angela out of the house. Instead, Ruby left and spent a couple weeks visiting with long-time friends and soul searching. Finally, Ruby came to the conclusion that if Jesus wouldn't condemn Angela, then she didn't have the right to either.

It turned out to be a beautiful, powerful reunion so that everyone was bawling, including Angela's four-year old, Cole, who had no idea why he was crying. By now, Pastor Miller had been such a presence in the Chiccone's lives that Cole had practically forgotten his former existence when Ray wasn't around. They spent time together for special occasions besides Tuesday nights. They talked on the phone often. And Cole was attaching himself to Ray as the father figure he never knew he needed.

Which worked out fine, because the pastor knew nothing about being a father.

So, when Cole invited Ray to his birthday party coming up that weekend, it was only natural for him to say, "Of course I'll be there." That's when Angela warned, "We're havin' it at the youth center at Cole's school."

"Ok," Ray commented as if to say, 'So?'

"They are celebratin' every kid who has a birthday in March."

"Are you trying to get me to change my mind?"

Angela rolled her eyes and smirked, "I'm preparin' you for the chaos. There will be lots of kids there." Then another thought struck her. "Kids with normal family members…" she looked at her feet, "like mothers and…"

Raymond interrupted, "I can assure you, Angela, in today's day and age families are anything *but* normal." He turned to tousle her son's hair. "Besides, I think Cole's 'family' will be well represented."

Cole simply beamed.

Pastor Miller decided to cover the book of Romans as a natural progression to John in their Tuesday night Bible study. As usual, all three generations of the Chiccones were present in the small but comfortable living room – Cole having coloring books or drawing pads to keep him occupied. Raymond began tonight with Chapter one. Their tradition was to read the whole chapter and then study it verse by verse.

Tonight, Angela following along, saw something which jumped out at her when Ray got to verses 16,

17, & 18. "Wait a sec, Ray. What is the 'gospel of Christ'?"

"Remember the teaching in John where God sent Jesus into the world so that whoever believes in Him will not perish, but have everlasting life?"

"Yeah?"

"Well that's pretty much the whole gospel."

"Then what does it mean in verse 17, 'For in it the righteousness of God is revealed,' and then in 18, 'the wrath of God is revealed?' It's still talkin' about the gospel, right?"

Ray was impressed. "Wow! That's good you picked up on that. Ok, the John 3:16 verse is the short version of the gospel. The long story goes like this: because of all the sin in the earth – and we are going to see a list of some as we continue reading – God's wrath, His hatred of sin, means He had to judge the earth because everywhere all men sin."

"Everybody sins so everybody gets judged."

"That's correct. There's no way around it. But the other side of the gospel is that Jesus took God's punishment on Himself."

"But you told us Jesus never sinned," Ruby commented.

"Also correct, Ruby. So then why was Jesus punished?"

She thought a moment and then her face brightened. Ruby gasped, "He took the punishment that was meant for us!?!"

Raymond grinned, "Exactly! We were sinners and Jesus took our judgment so that we could take on the righteousness of sinless Jesus. Do you see it?"

Angela, reading ahead, then asked, "So what does the next verse mean? 'Because what may be known of God is manifest in them…' I thought the gospel 'revealed.' Now its sayin' that people do? I'm so confused," she confessed while furrowing her brow.

"I should have warned you before we started that Romans is full of… terminologies you'll understand once you learn more."

"So you're sayin' I'm too stupid to understand this stuff, now?"

"Of course not! We've been studying less than six months and have barely scratched the surface. It has nothing to do with your ability to learn."

Angela's frustration clearly manifested itself on her face. She was seeing something in the scriptures he read and desperately wanted to understand. And she said so, "Then start explainin' it, Raymond."

Ray sighed and set down his Bible. "Ok, maybe it would be better if I summarized what Romans 1 is saying."

She steeled her gaze at him.

"Right. Think of it this way." Raymond fortified himself and matched her steady stare. "You are a life that reflects the glory of God."

This broke Angela's intensity momentarily, but she kept steady.

He continued, "Whether or not you accept the gospel message, God is going to get His glory through you."

"What!?!" asked Angela, clearly shocked. "How can you say all those years when I was…" she glanced down at Cole, "all those years when I was sinnin' that I was bringin' glory to God?"

"Angela, God uses *everyone* to reveal His glory to the world. Tell me… we just learned that God's wrath needs to judge us for our sins, right?"

"Yeah?"

"Well, was God justified? Did He have every right to judge you for your sins?"

Angela slumped in her seat, folded her hands in her lap and stared at them. In a quiet voice she answered, "Yes, He did."

Ruby perked up. She placed a hand on her daughter's forearm. "But He didn't! Don't you see? He judged Jesus for your sins."

Angela placed her fingers on her forehead and pondered. "So, God gets His glory by judgin' me for my sins, but He gets His glory by *not* condemnin' me for my sins?"

Raymond nodded his head. "Right! God gets to show the world who He is by punishing people for their sins. OR, if they choose to believe in Jesus, by giving us Jesus' righteousness. Either way, God gets all the glory."

Feeling overwhelmed, Angela sat back on the sofa. "Whoa," was all she could come up with.

"I couldn't have said it better myself," agreed Pastor Miller.

On an unusually warm day mid-Spring, Pastor Miller and his faithful Head Usher Earl Barclay were at the church waiting for the exterminator. Every year about this time, they purchased a preventive spray in order to avoid having a problem with ants. It was actually Brother Barclay's idea, which they implemented three years ago. So, he was here to show the professionals where to spray. While waiting, they talked.

"I think it's a fine thang, you doin' for that Ang-la and her fam-ly, Pastuh. A fine thang indeed!" the elderly black man praised.

"Yes, brother. But there are times when I don't feel like I'm getting anywhere with them."

"Oh, you cain't think thata way, Pastuh."

"But they don't even come to church!"

"They'll git to chu-ch when they's ready. But that's not what I'm meanin'."

"Well… what is it, then?"

"You bein' *involved*, Pastuh! You's a preacher man… a *good* preacher man. But you's a *man*! You take my meanin' yet?"

Raymond's face reddened as he stifled a smile. He bowed his head, placing his fist to his mouth as if about to clear his throat. "I'm being a friend, Brother Barclay. That's all."

"Oh, Pastuh! You ain't lookin' at it from where *I'm* standin'. You's bein' a fam-ly man."

He threw his head back and laughed. "Oh-ho-ho-kay. This is where this conversation needs to come to an end."

"What're you ashamed of Pastuh? You got the complete package all under one roof. All's you got to do is seal the deal!"

Pastor Miller was spared from any more embarrassment as the exterminator truck pulled into the parking lot. "Ok, brother. Time to get to work, now."

Later that night, Ray pondered before he fell asleep. "Lord, are you trying to tell me something through my conversation with Brother Barclay? Is he really seeing something I should be?" And as he closed his eyes he made a commitment to keep them open.

The next Tuesday night, Pastor Miller showed up to the Chiccone's as usual, "Come on in, Ray.

Angela isn't back with Cole from his doctor's appointment, yet." Ruby explained.

"Doctor's appointment? Is everything alright?"

Ms. Chiccone laughed, "Of course. It's just a well-child visit. You know… a check-up? Remember having those when you were a kid?"

Ray laughed nervously, "Ha, I guess it *has* been a while. Maybe her not being here is providential."

"What do you mean?"

"What do you know about Cole's father?"

"You mean sperm donor."

Ray tsk'd.

"That's all he was; a flash in the pan. In the door, out the door. Angela may have had a whole two-week relationship with the guy. Nothing serious."

"So, she *does* know who the father is!"

"Get something straight, Raymond." Ruby seethed. Now he knew where her daughter got it from. "She knows *who* Cole's father is, but she doesn't *know* his father."

"Let me guess, he's denying all involvement."

"Denying!?! Try non-existent! As in, he won't acknowledge our existence at all."

"That's tragic," Ray lamented.

"Good Lord, Raymond. Angela's life is filled with one tragedy after another. You are the first man — no, wait — the first *person* to ever take an interest in her."

"Well, God led me to her. Or more accurately, God led her to me. I care deeply about her soul — comes with the occupation," he grinned.

"I think you care about more than just her soul, Ray."

'Oh, no,' thought Ray, 'not another one,' "What do you mean?" he asked naively.

"I've seen how you look at her… how you let your guard down when you are around her."

"I'm sorry… I didn't…"

"Oh, stop apologizing, Raymond, It's only natural. But let me finish. I've also seen how Angela behaves around you! She's been hurt by so many people – men mostly. So, it's like she doesn't know how to act. I guess she's trying to feel you out – you know… see if your caring is genuine. Then she'll let *her* guard down."

"That's quite an insight, Ruby. I don't know how to take it."

Ruby grinned, "You don't have to *do* anything, Ray. Just keep being yourself and caring about my daughter." At this point she winked, "At least *one* of us knows you are the genuine article."

Ray smiled sheepishly and his face felt hot. In fact, he felt so uncomfortable that by the time Angela walked in she had to ask, "What's the matter, Ray?" Fear was creeping into her voice.

He laughed nervously. "Nothing, Angela. Your mother was just confirming how clueless I am to the Chiccone culture.

She furrowed her brow. "What the heck does that mean?"

"I keep coming over here week after week and we've learned so much about the Bible and God. But I know very little about you, your family, and you know very little about me." Angela relaxed and looked at her mother as if to say, 'Where's he going with this?'

Ruby ratted him out, "Ray was asking about Cole's father."

Cole piped up with a statement which sounded like he was reciting by rote. "I don't have a dad. He's dead."

Angela stiffened and turned red at her son's lie. She then shrugged her shoulders and justified, "It's the simplest explanation."

Ray's heart immediately went out to her in empathy. He swallowed a lump. "I understand."

Ruby intervened. "What do you say we just have a regular evening tonight? We'll order pizza and spend the time getting to know each other."

Thankful for the tension breaker, Ray said, "I'm game if you are." He looked to Angela.

Angela appeared as though she were the target of a conspiracy. But she relented. "I'm ok with it."

The evening actually progressed much smoother than it started. So much so that Angela felt more comfortable than at any time she could remember.

Ray opened up first; he more or less gave his testimony. He grew up in the drug experimenting eighties and he tried them all. At some point, while the rest of his friends settled on a drug they wanted to grow old with, Ray decided he had grown out of the mood enhancers. He didn't find God yet, that was later. But he became restless. Just like he bounced around with drugs, he jumped from relationship to relationship, job to job, etc.

It was actually his parents who were able to pin him down. Mr. and Mrs. Miller (who have since retired to the Midwest dry heat of Arizona) found God and introduced Him to Ray. He discovered the solid foundation he'd been looking for and, well… never looked back. He was so sold out, he enrolled in seminary. Ray's Southern Baptist Church was the first place he landed after graduating eight years ago and he's been there ever since.

Ruby and Angela tag-teamed their stories. Like Ruby had warned, it was one tragedy after another. The elder Chiccone was raised in a solid homestead; church going folks. But she met a man who swept her off her feet. Ruby got pregnant before getting married, so her parents disowned her. After Angela was born, they wed but it was rocky from the start. Stuart Chiccone announced as he was walking out the front door, "I'm going down to the corner store to pick up a few things. I probably won't be back."

Ruby wasn't surprised, She saw it coming and steeled herself for it ahead of time. She took her young daughter back to Mom and Dad's and reconciled. They have since passed on. She went to school and got a career in a medical office. Because she had to work a lot of hours, she left Angela on her own who proved early on that she was able to raise herself. So, Ruby let her… asking no questions. Angela chose prostitution simply because she was good at it. It paid the bills. Word of mouth got around; she got kicked out of school and never finished. For all those years, Ruby thought she was waitressing (which, Angela admitted, is not that much different from prostitution. "The type of service is the only difference," she said with a laugh. "I'll never look at a waitress the same again," admitted Ray).

Things got tough when she got pregnant. She had no insurance and couldn't work. But because Ruby worked in the medical field, Angela was able to have a healthy baby Cole at a significant discount. Now Angela was responsible for two lives. She got back to work.

By now, Cole had fallen asleep on the couch and Ray volunteered to carry him to his bed. He gingerly picked up the husky five-year old and carried him off to his room. When he came back, Angela was in the living room by herself. "Momma went to bed, too."

"Am I overstaying my welcome?"

"No, this is actually kinda fun. I think she just wanted to give us a chance to… uh… I don't know the words for it."

Ray smirked, "I think I understand," he admitted as he sat next to her on the couch. "So tell me about your love life."

Angela glared at him. "That's not even funny, Raymond."

Not wavering he added, "Oh, come on; in all those years you never had a gentleman suitor? Nobody fell in love with you?"

"Love?" she crowed in her deep southern drawl. "Ha! I wouldn't know what that looked like if it bit me in the butt! The only love I've ever managed to muster is completely spent on Cole. He's my life."

"So, are you saying there's no room for anyone else?"

"I'm just sayin' I wouldn't even know where to start."

"I don't think it needs to be any big mystery," Ray explained as though sure of himself. "Just follow your heart."

Angela smirked. "Follow my heart, huh? Is that the best you can come up with?"

Visibly uncomfortable, Ray continued, "Well, I'm no expert but that is what *I'm* trying to do." And with that he dropped his guard completely, leaned over and kissed her.

Angela let it go on for a couple of seconds, then pulled away. She stiffened up, clearly shaken. "What's the matter?" asked Ray.

"I don't know…" she confessed.

"Was I really that bad?" he gushed, feeling stupid.

"No, Ray, it wasn't the kiss. I just… I feel…" Angela was stumped. She had never felt those kinds of feelings before, and it overwhelmed her. "I'm feeling overwhelmed."

"Overwhelmed?"

"Yeah, can we call it a night?" She switched into courteous hostess mode. "I really had a nice time. I'm glad you stayed."

Disappointed, Ray played along. "Yeah, I had a nice time as well. This was a great idea Ruby had."

Angela walked him to the door. "Yeah, it was. We'll have to do it again."

Ray searched her eyes, but Angela's fortress had completely closed up for the night. "Yeah, goodnight Angela."

"Goodnight Raymond."

As she closed the door, they both realized they had some evaluating to do tonight.

They had no contact for the week. But Ray showed up the next Tuesday night as usual for Bible study.

The Chiccones were cordial, and the evening went smoothly. But heart issues were not discussed. *And* both Angela and Ruby seemed guarded tonight. Ray felt like he was being left out of something important, but he didn't ask about it. He figured they would let him know when it was time.

Then came the call on Thursday afternoon. Ray was in his church office when the phone rang.

"Pastor Miller here."

"Ray?" It was Ruby. "Do you think you could come over here?"

"Is anything wrong?"

She sounded as if she were trying to fight the urgency in her voice. "I'd rather not discuss it over the phone."

"Ok, Ruby, give me 20 minutes."

"Ray? I don't think you have 20 minutes."

He dropped the phone on his desk and flew from his office.

When he arrived, the front door was open, and Angela was arguing with her mother. He couldn't hear what was being said, but a quick survey showed him a vehicle loaded with personal belongings – Cole sitting in the front seat. He waved to Ray.

Ray returned the wave and ran to the front door. "What's going on?"

"There, see?" Ruby said, "He's here."

"I can see that, Momma."

"You at least owe him an explanation."

Angela huffed and Ruby walked away to give them privacy.

Ray waited. He didn't want to say anything even though his heart was pounding out of his chest.

Before she faced him, Angela steadied herself. Then she took a deep breath and *steeled* herself.

She turned and exclaimed, "I *have* to do this, Ray!"

Ray acknowledged, "Ok… do what?"

"I'm leavin'."

'I can see that,' Ray thought, but didn't want to sound condescending. Instead he simply asked, "Why?"

"Because I have to," she reiterated.

"Ok, but help me understand, Angela."

Angela relaxed a little. "I ain't sure I can explain it myself. There's just too much here. This is where I grew up. I need to get away from it – from *all* of it."

"So that you can…" he prompted.

"Ugh!" she screeched. "You just ain't gonna let up, are you? You're gonna make me say this." Ray steadied himself, "Whatever you have to say, it needs to be said." He left it at that.

Angela moistened her lips and then looked him in the eyes. "I've been following you, Ray, all this time. You led me out of my life of sin. But now it's time to find my own way."

"And I'm not allowed to help you anymore?"

"This is somethin' I gotta do on my own. Remember you once told me I am a life that reflects the glory of God?"

"Yes."

"Well, let me."

"Let you what?"

"Let me reflect God's glory. I can't reflect Ray's glory of God. All my life I've been on autopilot just doin' what I had to... to get by. Well, God has a purpose for me. I know that now. And I need to find out what that is."

"I still don't understand why you have to go away to figure out what that is."

"I have to get away from my life, Ray. From everythin' that's familiar. It's clouding my vision. It's in the way so I can't see God."

"Am I in your way?"

"Especially you, Ray!" she practically shouted. Then she backed off and put a gentle hand on his arm. "Ray, you already hear from God. He's already told you what He wants from you. I need to hear Him for myself... without distraction."

Ray bowed his head because he knew she was making perfect sense. And he said as much.

"You're right, Angela, I should know better. Perhaps my vision is clouded, too."

She kissed his forehead, "I'm not gonna say goodbye because that's forever. So... I'll see you around, Raymond."

"For what it's worth…" he pointed to where he was standing, "I'll be here when you get back."

"That's worth somethin', Ray. It's worth a lot."

Out of the Comfort Zone

A Sunday morning like no other…

Usually Pastor Raymond Miller preached with such fire. Not fire and brimstone, mind you. But you could tell when he preached that he loved his job. Except for this particular Sunday morning. His message, while completely accurate as always, left his parishioners wondering if the fire was going out. Perhaps that wasn't so far from the truth. Pastor Miller's head usher Earl Barclay confronted him about it after service ended and everyone left.

"Feel like talkin', Pastuh?" the elderly black man inquired.

"About what, Barclay?" Raymond countered.

"Now, I think you know what I'm wonderin' about. The chu-ch folks is concerned. Yer not yerself today."

"Oh, that," he paused. After a deep breath he confronted Barclay. "You almost had me convinced."

"To what are you referrin'?"

"You know. I was content with my lot in life. Sure, I've always wondered about marriage – who hasn't? But I figured God would cover that ground with me when I was ready. Until then, I was fine with being single."

"And where do I come in?" asked Barclay.

"Well, thanks to you putting that idea in my head about 'the complete package all under one roof,' I allowed my heart to get carried away by that woman."

"Seems to me that's yer *problem*, Pastuh."

"What do you mean by that, Barclay?"

"You gave your heart to Jesus, din't ya'?"

"Of course!"

"Well, what're you doin' takin' it back to give it to some woman?"

Convicted, Pastor Miller conceded. "Excellent point, Barclay. But I thought you told me you saw something in my relationship with Angela, so I figured I was going to spend the rest of my life with her."

"What makes you think you ain't?"

"She left, Barclay. She's gone… left home. Left me."

"And she said she ain't comin' back?"

"Well, no… but"

"Jus' hang in there, Pastuh. You never know what God's got up His sleeve," he advised with a huge grin.

The dust had finally settled.

At first, Angela Chiccone and her five-year old son, Cole, had no idea where they were going… or what they were going to do when they got there.

Her friend Raymond Miller told her one time, "follow your heart," so she followed it to Alabama – two states away! She entered a quaint little town just over the border and was immediately reminded why she was doing this in the first place. Angela was seeking God's direction for her life. So it was to Him she turned just now. "Lord, show me where to go." The idea struck her like a rock upside her head.

She didn't have to search very far, this being the Bible Belt and all. She turned onto tree-lined 'Church Street' and followed it to a clearing at the end. When she saw it, she grinned.

"Looks like we're here, Cole."

"Where? Cole perked up from his drawing pad to peer out the window.

"We're goin' to church."

"What's church?"

Angela forgot. Cole had never been to church. Oh sure, Raymond showed up every Tuesday to do Bible studies with her and her mom, Ruby. So, Cole knew about God. But he's never stepped one foot into church,

"It's kinda like God's house," she explained.

"I get to see where God lives?" he asked, excited.

Angela chuckled. "No, honey. God lives in your heart. Church is where people go to learn about God."

"Oh." Then he thought a moment. "I like learning about God from Ray."

She cringed, but Cole wouldn't know what that was all about. She hid it anyway with her words. "I do too, Cole."

"Why can't Ray come with us?"

Angela sighed and opened her door. "Well, because we're already here." That was two weeks ago.

There was a new face in the congregation Sunday morning.

Ray saw Ruby Chiccone right away when he stepped up to the pulpit. It created such a stir in him that he preached with the same vigor for which he was known.

 After service, he had to wait while several of his parishioners welcomed Ruby with handshakes and hugs. Apparently, his rebuke all those months ago about not treating strangers like family was still having an impact.

When it was finally his turn, Ray announced beaming, "Ruby! To what do I owe this pleasant surprise?"

"Well, for one, I miss you, Raymond." Then she crouched and looked around. "Is it alright for me to call you 'Raymond' in church? Or am I supposed to say 'Reverend' or something?"

Pastor Miller laughed. "No, no. It's perfectly acceptable. We're *all* family here." Then conviction set in. "I'm sorry I stopped coming on Tuesday nights. After Angela left I didn't… I just didn't think I had it in me. But after seeing you this morning," he brightened, "I would love to continue."

"Well, I wish you would. Like you said, 'we're family!' Do you know what it's like to not hear from your kid in two or three weeks!?! Excruciating! Which brings me to the second reason I'm here."

"Which is?"

"I thought you would want to know. I heard from Angela."

Raymond's heart skipped a beat. He was unable to hide his excitement from her mother, though.

"What did she say?"

"Well… do you have plans for lunch? I thought we could eat and discuss it."

"I do now! What did you have in mind?"

"Take me home, Raymond," she beamed. "I have a roast in the oven."

It was the same Sunday morning…

And Angela felt just as uncomfortable today as she did the first Sunday; even though she was getting to know the people. Plus, she even looked like them, (some of the ladies had donated a few dresses so she would have nice things to dress up in. Cole was wearing a little suit someone had given him explaining their child had outgrown it). It just didn't feel like… well, like home yet.

"I hit a skunk," the pastor began. Pastor and Mrs. Thoms were pivotal in helping Angela get established in town. They seemed to understand why she was doing what she was doing. They believed God sent her to them, so they pledged to help make Angela's transition as seamless as possible.

Pastor Thoms explained the skunk story and related how he had quite a mess to clean up on his vehicle. Well, the car wash did an excellent job of removing any sign of carcass. However, as with any skunk accident, you are left with overwhelming evidence… that is to say, the smell. "And you can *still* smell it when you walk out in the parking lot!

"Well, sin is a lot like that. We come to Christ, turn our lives over to God and He promises to 'forgive us our sins and cleanse us from all unrighteousness' according to I John 1:9. The carcass of the old man is removed from us just as cleanly and efficiently as the car wash did the dead skunk!

"But we are left with the memories of our past. We still have to deal with the guilt and the shame of our old lives. And the 'stink' seems to penetrate everything we try to do and become."

Angela was enrapt. Fighting back tears, she could relate to everything Pastor Thoms was saying. She knew exactly how paralyzing the shame was. You don't just walk away from a life of prostitution without baggage. It even affected her attempt to become a normal, productive member of society.

The pastor went on to explain that whether we realize it or not, God is capable of cleansing us from all the guilt, shame, grief, whatever, as well. It's *we* who hold onto stuff. Then, beginning with Psalm 51, he rattled off one scripture after another describing God wiping away all guilt and iniquity. At the end of his sermon, Pastor Thoms offered the altar up front for those who wished to be cleansed of all their guilt and shame. Angela practically ran to the front.

When service was over, Mrs. Thoms – who had been praying with and embracing Angela – asked her if she would like to come over for Sunday dinner.

"I'd love to," expressed Angela, showing disappointment. "But I've gotta go to work."

"Work!" Raymond Miller was shocked out of his too-full-and-feeling-guilty reverie. "All those months looking for work here and coming up with nothing. She's out there barely three weeks and she's already got a job?"

Ruby Chiccone nodded. "Which tells me that whatever this is she's doing is in God's hands."

Ray pondered this while Ruby continued. In his heart he really wanted to please God. But that same heart was really missing his friend.

"Apparently, there's a fancy restaurant in town that needed a hostess. The pastor of the church Angela goes to knows the owner. Well, you know Angela! She turned on the charm and the restaurant owner practically begged her to come work for him."

Ray laughed to himself remembering what Angela had said about the only difference between a prostitute and a waitress is the type of service provided. He recapped, "So, she's got a job, the church folks… which still shocks me. I mean, she wouldn't even come to church while she was here!"

"Yes, Raymond, but you know the reason for that."

"I know, I know, She didn't want to have me as her pastor."

"That's right. She likes you, Ray. She didn't want to have to act differently around you."

"So, she's going to this church in, where'd you say? Alabama?"

"Yep."

"And they found her an apartment, loaded her up with clothes and other necessities. What else is there?"

"Well, in a couple weeks Cole will be starting first grade."

Ray humphed. He really missed Angela. But he'd been getting attached to her only child, too. Ray had no idea how to be a dad and Cole never knew his father. But the two of them seemed to hit it off from day one.

He got up from the table. "It seems God has all her bases covered. The only thing you haven't mentioned is her love life."

"I didn't mention it, because Angela didn't mention it. It's only been three weeks, Raymond."

"You're right. I'm behaving like a love-sick schoolboy."

"I don't think you have anything to worry about, Ray. She had to take this adventure, but I'm positive God is just using it to put things into perspective *for* Angela because she couldn't do it herself. You're still going to be a part of her life. She just needs to see it for herself."

Ray turned to face his friend. "Where did you acquire all this wisdom? *I'm* usually the one doing all the counseling."

Ruby waved him off. "Wisdom of years, Ray. Remember, I'm *much* older than you."

"I wouldn't say *much* older." He grabbed her hands.

"But you also have to remember you are very much a man. And a lonely man at that."

"I never really considered myself lonely."

"Only because you were used to your routine, Ray. Just like Angela you were so blinded by the familiar you couldn't see God attempting to 'expand your world' so to speak."

Embracing Ruby he confessed, "So, by Angela leaving, maybe God had to shake up my world, too?"

"I think so." She pulled away and looked up at him. "So, I'll see you Tuesday?"

Ray smiled. "I'd like that."

The routine of small-town life.

Angela was really getting into it: quaint little church, dropping Cole off at school, parent/teacher conferences, everybody knows everybody. But most of all, she had a normal job… with a paycheck… paying taxes!

And hostessing for Mr. Carmichael *almost* seemed to be her calling in life. 'Almost,' Angela thought to herself. She was so good at greeting people, making them feel comfortable and genuine 'Southern hospitality.' But at the same time she knew it wasn't really her. Every day she got dressed up, assumed this character and put on a performance which both men and women came to enjoy.

At the end of the day, it made her feel guilty thinking about it. It's not that she wasn't appreciative to God for the person she was becoming, but that she got to hide behind it. Nobody knew where she came from; the life she left behind. And they didn't question her about it! Everyone just immediately accepted her when she came to town. She was drowning in love and didn't know whether to sink to the bottom or swim to shore.

In the meantime, she was enjoying the attention. Women would complement. Men would flirt – and she always had a remark to put them in their place. A favorite line she used whenever awestruck gentlemen would say, "Aw, Angela, when are you going to settle down and marry me?" was, "My heart already belongs to somebody else… Jesus." This brought a hearty 'AMEN!'

One Sunday, an announcement was made about a women's brunch taking place on Tuesday.

'Huh… Tuesday,' pondered Angela as she remembered the significance of that day. She wondered if her mother was still carrying on the weekly tradition with Raymond. Just the thought of his name struck a chord somewhere deep within her. So, she pushed the thought out of her mind and made plans to attend the brunch on Tuesday.

She walked into Sara Hopper's house bearing her dish-to-pass. Angela still wasn't comfortable exposing her cooking to the public, so she brought a tray of sliced fresh fruit.

"Oh, Angela!" Mrs. Hopper gushed as though she wasn't expecting her to show up. "I am sooo glad you're here."

"I wouldn't even think of missin' a girls' night out – even if it *is* during the day!" Angela countered in her traditional southern drawl.

"Well, we are certainly going to have a wonderful time. We'll have brunch, but I saved a surprise for everyone. I invited a guest speaker."

"A guest speaker? You mean we ain't gonna sit around and gossip?" Angela teased.

Sara Hopper laughed, "Absolutely not! Especially since that's what the men all think we're doing," she winked.

She led Angela out the back door onto the porch where the smorgasbord was laid out. The weather was perfect and still accommodating here in late October for an outdoor event such as this.

Mingling with the ladies, Angela got to meet and know some, which she barely recognized at church by name. At one point, the topic turned to gentlemen suitors. Angela wasn't the only single woman in attendance, but the women sat around assigning perfect matches. She laughed right along with the matchups. But she couldn't help feeling nervous when her name came up.

"What about our beloved Angela?"

"Oh, I don't want to play," knowing there was no way she was going to get out of it. Someone suggested, "It would have to be someone very popular." "Or someone highly respected," another added.

"I ain't marryin' no town mayor," Angela teased.

The women giggled until someone gasped, "I know…" she dragged out the word with a cat-ate the-canary grin. "How about Dr. Morris."

Most of the women blushed. Angela heard, "Oh, he's perfect," "Yeah, he's single," "He's so gentle," "Does he go to our church?" and "The gynecologist?" She wasn't smiling.

"Have you met him yet?" asked Kathy, who was sitting right next to her.

"No," Angela admitted, looking at her hands folded in her lap.

This caused Kathy to probe. "You mean you've been here this whole time and you haven't been checked, yet?"

Angela knew what that meant and decided she'd rather change the subject. "No. Does anyone want more coffee?"

The women ganged up on her. She had to have a check-up. Wasn't she concerned for her health? Dr. Morris is so gentle, (didn't someone say that before?) It's the responsible thing to do.

Angela gave away nothing. So Kathy offered, "How about I set up a meeting? You know, like an interview… during the day… at a public place. Where you could get to know each other first. See if he's someone you'd like to do business with."

Angela switched on the charm, "If I didn't know any better, Kathy, I'd swear you were tryin' to set me up on a date."

Kathy blushed, but the suggestion worked. Angela would have her meeting.

Over the course of the next couple months on Tuesday nights, Raymond heard news from Alabama. Most weeks there was nothing to report. But he heard about Angela's involvement with the ladies of the church. He beamed with pride as Ruby bragged about Cole learning to read and then helping to teach the other kids. He cringed when he heard that Angela had met a man – a doctor, no less - and had spent the Thanksgiving holiday with him.

There was a group of people there, but still… it rattled his faith.

So, when Ruby invited Ray to share Christmas with her on the Tuesday a week and a half before the actual holiday, it was only natural for him to accept. She was, after all, his best friend. Oh sure, he had lots of friends from his church (which is why Ruby invited him so early – he would be stretched thin the next few days by so many obligations). But for some reason *this* relationship thrived, because Ray was *not* affiliated with his church. Which was weird… but it worked.

Ray walked in with a platter of Christmas cookies (his secret favorite part of the holiday traditions). They shared a quiet evening… and the topic of Angela never came up. Ray could not even see any evidence that she had tried to contact her mother to send Christmas greetings.

Ruby distracted his reverie. "Raymond, do you know what my favorite part of the Christmas story is?"

"I don't believe we've ever discussed it."

"We haven't. But I will tell you anyway. The fact that it was just a regular day… you know, business as usual."

Ray humphed.

"Think about it. Nobody knew Jesus was coming… except of course his parents.

"Yeah, you're right. In fact, it was *so* busy they couldn't even stay in an inn. They had to spend the night with the animals. Imagine the accommodations everyone would have made if they knew their king was being born to them."

"Right! People were so oblivious, *angels* had to announce Jesus' coming!" Ray laughed and pondered this. Maybe he could use it in a sermon sometime.

Ruby continued. "You know? I think God still works like that today. We're just going on about our usual responsibilities, and then God sends His angels to make an announcement." She heard a door slam, then checked her watch. 'Just in time,' she thought. "Looks like He's sending us one, right now."

Ray watched her make her way to the front door. "What are you talking about?"

She ignored him. As she opened the door, she couldn't fight the tears as she heard, "Grandma!"

Ray shot to his feet, his heart beating out of his chest in excitement. He rushed to the door as Angela and Cole stepped in out of the cold. But he stopped dead in his tracks. 'Perhaps she's different and wouldn't want me here.'

But she saw him right away. She passed a package to her mother. "Hello, Raymond. You said you'd be here when I got back." She kissed Ruby, then made her way over to Ray and embraced him.

Angela inhaled his scent and declared, "Man, I missed you."

Ray was speechless… but managed in crackled voice, "So, does that mean you're back to stay?"

She pulled away and declared, "Looks that way."

He collapsed in his seat. Then he spied Ruby. "You knew all along, didn't you?"

Ruby shrugged her shoulders and grinned mischievously. She scooped her grandson up into her arms who then proceeded to cover her with kisses. "Grandma, I can read!"

"You can?" she exclaimed, sharing his excitement. "You'll have to read me something."

"Right now?"

"Sure!" She decided it would be best to give her daughter and friend some time together. "Do you remember where your room is?"

"Yeah!" he tore down the hall.

"Look at you! You look like you've grown a foot taller!"

When they were gone, Angela sat on the couch next to Ray's chair.

"So, Angel, do you have a message for me?" he smirked.

"Huh?" she questioned, confused.

"Something your mother said before you came in. How've you been? I haven't heard from you in what?" He checked his watch for the dramatic pause. "Four, five months?"

"Are you gonna scold me or would you like to learn what I discovered?"

"I'm sorry," he dropped his head, convicted. "Tell me your story."

"I guess the easiest way to start is by sayin' that I had to discover who I am by findin' out who I'm not."

"Makes sense to me."

"It does?"

"Sure. God makes us new creations. The best way to learn what the new man or woman is, is by learning what He wants us to let go of."

"Yeah! And I found out I ain't cut out for all that small-town, typical American household stuff. I liked bein' treated nice and discoverin' who God

wants me to be. But because my past was a secret…
well, it's easy to love a sweetheart."

"You didn't tell anyone about your past?"

"Not a soul. Well, I had the opportunity to but
didn't. I'll tell you about it in a minute. But that's
what made all those relationships so… I don't
know… shallow.

"I guess the best way to explain it is that Jesus knows
all about my sinful past AND He knows the new
Angela I'm tryin' to be, and He loves both! So, I had
to come back to the man who knows my past as well
as the new me… and loves both."

Ray's mouth dropped open. "Are you saying?"

Angela beamed and nodded her head. "That is… if
he'll have me."

"Oh, he'll have you. I mean, *I'll* have you. I mean,
I'll take you!" He threw open his arms. And she
dove into them. They held each other a long time…
until Ruby and Cole came back in.

"Well, I guess that's settled." Ruby declared. "Who
wants some of Ray's Christmas cookies?"

"I do!" shouted Cole.

Angela looked up. "You made Christmas cookies?"

He shrugged with a sheepish grin. They got up together and walked into the kitchen. Ruby was pouring milk and Angela sampled while Ray asked, "You said something about having an opportunity to tell someone about your past?"

Angela froze mid-chew and put a hand under her chin. "Oh, yeah." She grabbed a glass of milk and took a few swallows. It appeared as though she was trying to shore up her courage. "I met a doctor," she began.

"I heard," Ray spoke out of the corner of his mouth.

She gave him a scowl. "Anyway… the girls all bragged about this guy because he is a gynecologist. Well, I haven't been checked in like… well, since Cole was born.

"Anyway, I kept puttin' off getting checked, but I was meetin' with this guy so he would get to know me a little. That way he wouldn't freak out when he finally did give me an exam."

"Did it work?"

"You bet! He was really gentle, but he had to give me *all* the tests because I ain't been in so long.

When he was done, you could tell he was uncomfortable. It made *me* uncomfortable. He said to me, 'Angela, it looks like you've experienced some… trauma.' He paused just like that, and I think I actually jumped. But he said, 'Now, you don't have to tell me anything that's happened to you. But if you do, it'll make it easier to diagnose what's going on inside you.'"

"And you decided not to tell him."

"Yep. I shook my head, 'no,' and he sighed. That's when he gave me the bad news."

"What bad news?" asked Ruby. "You didn't tell me there was any bad news!"

"This ain't the kinda thing you talk about on the phone, Momma. Anyway…" she paused, swallowing tears. "I'm not gonna be able to have any more kids."

"Oh, honey," consoled Ruby, placing a hand on her forearm.

"And I'm probably gonna have to have a hysterectomy."

There was a long, deafening silence. Then, "Are you sure?" asked Ruby.

Angela exhaled as though she'd been holding her breath this whole time. Nodding her head she said, "Pretty sure."

They gathered in a little circle and held each other until the tears passed. Then Angela folded herself up as though trying to hide the shame and disgust from her past all over again. She looked sheepishly up at Ray and asked, "So… do you still want me?"

Ray coughed, "Of course I do! What kinda question is that!?!" And they embraced again, tears flowing a second time.

Cole asked, "Are you guys gonna cry all night?"

This caused everyone to laugh and it lightened the mood a little. Ruby grabbed the tray of cookies and led the troop back into the living room.

Angela put her arm around her man and said, "But this means you won't have any kids of your own."

Ray stiffened and looked at her. "What are you talking about!?! I already do!" reaching down and tousling Cole's hair.

The Lesson

"Dear Lord, I don't know where to go with this. I'm excited; I'm scared; I'm not sure I even want to take this step. So, I guess I'll start with what I know… I know You! And I'm grateful for the relationship I have with You. All this time it's been just You and me. But now there's someone else in the picture. Don't get me wrong, I'm grateful You've put Angela into my life… and Ruby… and Cole. But the permanence, God… the work of a lifelong relationship-building with this woman! I want it, yes, I want it. It's just right now I'm feeling that taking on a wife is going to take away from You. Of course, maybe I'm wrong. Show me, Lord. I love You. Amen."

December 25th is usually pretty mild weather for Kentucky. But not this year. A Canadian cold front worked its way down from the north bringing a bitter chill. Leading up to Christmas the temperature dropped a little each day. When it landed, the thermometer hovered around 10 degrees; with the wind it was minus 10. "Too cold to snow," Brother Earl Barclay observed.

But the warmth inside – a warmth which only Christmas can inspire – made it terribly easy to forget what was happening outside.

The ten days prior, which took place in the combined lives of the Chiccones, and Raymond Miller were filled with more activity than you would think was humanly possible to squeeze into 240 hours – not accounting for sleep. Pastor Miller's schedule had already been laid out for him, so Angela decided it would be best if he just stuck to it and didn't interfere. She had her own crazy schedule. While Ray was ministering to the poor, she was scheduling and attending a doctor's appointment for a second opinion. (It was surprisingly easy to find a gynecologist during the Christmas season). While Pastor Miller was celebrating with various members of his congregation, she was decorating, shopping, and preparing to make Christmas nice for her five-year old son, Cole. But the two lovebirds made a pact to call each other every night before they went to sleep – no matter how late it was – falling asleep in each other's arms, over the phone.

So when everyone gathered December 25th in Ruby Chiccone's house, the holiday almost felt anticlimactic in comparison to the rest of the season. And since there was so much catching up to do… Well, let me try to explain the sequence of events.

After the night of the reunion, Ruby began setting in motion ideas for a wedding ceremony. These ideas were suddenly accelerated to plans when Angela returned home from her doctor's appointment. She told her mother (and eventually Ray as well) that she wanted to get married as a whole person before her scheduled hysterectomy, ("If we wait 'til after, Ray might have second thoughts"). The doctor was adamant about cutting her open as soon as possible, confirming Dr.

Morris' previous diagnosis. "How soon?" asked Ruby. "January 22nd," replied Angela. "Oh my," declared Ruby. While for the average person this could seem like a nightmare, for Ruby Chiccone, the Organized, it was a welcomed challenge. Skills she had developed by working in a medical office came in quite handy. Preliminary plans were developed to be presented to Raymond on Christmas night.

Now, Ray was oblivious to the whole thing. The closest he had ever been to wedding plans was "What time do I show up to church?" He had no idea what all went into a wedding. So, when they told him Saturday, January 20th on the phone one night, he simply shrugged and said, "Ok."

"Plus, you've gotta be thinkin' about a best man," explained Angela.

"That's easy," declared Ray, "My head usher, Brother Barclay."

After a pause Angela instructed, "Momma says bring him with you Christmas evening."

Fortunately, Brother Barclay was to be alone that night. His wife had gotten a head start to heaven several years prior, so he was actually looking forward to a quiet evening. Pastor Miller approached him about going to celebrate Christmas with the Chiccones. *And* the fact that they will be discussing wedding plans.

"Whad'ya need me fer, Pastuh?" asked the elderly black gentleman.

"I can't help thinking about having the complete package all under one roof," teased Raymond.

Brother Barclay grinned, "Now whar have I heard that b-fore?"

After a short observation of festivities on Christmas night, they got down to business… the entire wedding party present: groom, bride, maid-of-honor, best man and ring bearer. ("We need younger friends," Angela whispered to Ray).

But the first person addressed was Cole. "Cole, what do you think about the idea of Ray bein' your daddy?" asked his mother.

"I don't have a dad. He's dead," Cole recited as programmed.

And also as programmed, Angela cringed at the lie. "That's right, honey. So, would you like Ray to be your daddy?"

Cole looked up at Ray and Ray flashed a bright smile. Without changing expression he turned to his mother and said, "Yeah, I guess that'd be alright. But can I stay here and live with you?"

Ray guffawed. Ruby burst out laughing. Angela just smiled and picked up her son. "Well, of course you're gonna live with me. But I'm gonna go live at Ray's house."

"Can Grandma live with us?"

"Grandma has her own house."

"But you can come back to see me anytime you want," Ruby threw in.

Cole dropped his head and muttered, "Okay." He climbed off Angela's lap and went to his room.

"He'll get used to the idea," Ruby encouraged.

"Ok," Angela began, taking charge. "My operation is on Monday, January 22nd. So, the best time to get married is Saturday, January 20th."

"Ok," said Ray.

"Where are we gonna get married?"

"Ray grinned, "I know where there's a church available."

A look of disappointment crossed Angela's face. "I don't think that's such a good idea, Ray."

"Why not?" he countered.

"Well, because those are all *your* people. I ain't got no friends there," she volleyed in her southern drawl.

"You gots me," offered Brother Barclay.

Angela smiled, "Yes, but besides you."

"What did you have in mind?"

"Someplace neutral. We're startin' a new life... together. It cain't be that familiar."

"But all my parishioners... they'll want to see me get married... to celebrate with us."

"But I don't know those people."

"Ray?" interjected Ruby. "You've been here, you said, eight years? Is that right?"

"That's correct."

"And your profession has opened doors for you to get to know lots of people, right?"

"I guess you could say that."

"Well, Angela's been in this community her whole life. And her profession has given her somewhat of a reputation as well."

Simultaneously both Ray and Angela looked into their respective laps. Both remembering her being a prostitute at the town truck stop... which is where they met. (But that's another story :)

"All I'm saying is that she doesn't have friends like you do."

"I understand," Ray said, looking up at her. "What do you suggest?"

"How about a private ceremony? But then we do a reception where all your friends can celebrate with you."

Ray thought for a moment, "I like it. That way they can welcome her into the family all over again."

At that moment, Cole came walking out with an armload of toys, some clothes in a bag and his blanket. "I'm ready."

Angela turned. "Ready for what, honey?"

"To go live with Ray."

Everyone laughed and Ruby got up to assist Cole. "You don't have to go right now, Cole. You get to stay with Grandma a few more days." She led him back to his room still laughing.

"Dear Lord, I'm torn. But this time it's not between You and my fiancee. It's between Angela and my congregation. What am I going to tell them!?! Is she going to make me leave the church after we get married because they aren't her friends? I thought the Southern Baptist Church was my calling. Or are you calling me someplace else because I'm getting married?

The next couple of weeks bustled… which was reminiscent of the days prior to Christmas – but without all the holiday stuff. As it turns out, thanks to December 26th retail efforts to keep the public spending money, there were bargains to be found in the jewelry stores. Angela and Ray spent the whole day shopping for rings and finally settled on a matching set. Simple white gold bands, (engraved for free) with the engagement ring displaying a ½ carat diamond housed in a platinum setting.

The following Sunday, Ray made the announcement of his nuptials to his congregation. The Lord instructed him exactly what to say and not only was everyone completely understanding of the delicate position Angela was in, but many also came forward and pledged assistance. "Do you need a caterer?" "Want to borrow my limo?" "Does Angela have a gown?" "Where are you getting married?" The last question being the greatest mystery of all. (In the end, due to Pastor Miller's "celebrity" status, the two were married in an undisclosed location. Oh! and a honeymoon – when Angela felt strong enough – to Arizona to introduce her to his parents).

Ray took all these offers back to his future wife and mother-in-law. They sorted through what they decided they could use. Ray was left with, "What time do you want me there?"

There would be no fancy gowns or tuxes. Ray and Barclay would dress semi-formally but comfortably. Angela and her mother would wear matching dresses – light blue.

Ray called in his friend and mentor from the seminary in Ohio, Professor/Pastor Oliver Tussel.

Pastor Tussel was honored to be asked to officiate a wedding ceremony for one of his star pupils.

"Besides, there's nothing going on around here – it's Winter break."

Angela wanted a familiar face as well. She solicited help from her friends in Alabama, Pastor and Mrs. Thoms. They were delighted to be included. During their visit, Angela broke down (several times) and confessed her whole story to them; Ray holding her hand for support. They listened with rapt attention and when she finished they simply praised God for what He was doing with her and in her. Then they prayed for and blessed her, Ray and their union.

"Dear Lord, You are so incredible. I couldn't have asked for a more perfect setup to this marriage to a woman You have so obviously placed into my life for this purpose. I know Your hand is upon her to do with us what You want. I know you are guiding all the preparations and the wedding will take place with no problems. I know You are even now preparing the doctors, the hospital, and staff to provide for Angela a

peaceful surgery. I thank You for the grace that she and I should save ourselves and not lie together until after her surgery and recovery because, as Angela says it, "All the evidence of the old Angela will be completely removed" and I can have all the new Angela all to myself. I thank You for confidence that everything is going according to Your plan. I love You, Lord. I trust You. Amen."

The pastors tag-teamed and made the wedding ceremony beautiful. Ray's church outdid themselves for the reception. The day literally went better than planned. (Of course, on nearly everyone's wedding day something goes wrong. In the case of the Millers, no one scheduled any music for the reception – which everyone decided was an odd thing to forget. Angela suggested they have plenty of years to dance).

When it was over, the newly married Millers had a day and a half to get ready for surgery. And they needed every bit of those 30 some-odd hours. Pastor Tussel preached in Ray's church on Sunday morning, so Ray and his new bride could be absent. And the Thoms chaplained the Millers in preparation for not only the operation, but the aftereffects as well. "I had a hysterectomy, too," confessed Mrs. Thoms. "But I was much older than you are. So, the risks were much greater." She went on to explain what to expect in regard to her body, her hormones, her feelings, etc.

Angela was fine with all her faculties available to her. Well, she was fine until about noon on January 22nd.

Maybe it was nerves. She'd never had that much experience with doctors. The only time she was ever in a hospital was the morning Cole was born.

Maybe it was guilt. Through a life of promiscuity she allowed her body to be badly ravaged. Now it was rebelling, and she didn't want any part of it.

Or maybe it was the fact that she hadn't eaten anything in the past 12 hours in preparation for the operation. It was scheduled for 3 p.m.

But mostly it was her own rebellion. Angela questioned God why this could be happening to her.

"I don't want to do this, Ray," she determined.

"I don't think you have much choice, dear." Ray countered.

Angela steeled herself, which she'd always been good at. "It's my body and I'll do with it what I want." They were in the outer lobby waiting for their names to be called for pre-operation prepping. About that time, the Thoms showed up. They were there for support and to pray during the entire procedure. She saw them walk in. "Pastor Thoms, let's go have lunch somewhere."

He laughed, "Are you really that hungry after 12 hours?"

Ray exposed, "She's having second thoughts."

Pastor Thoms whispered something to his wife and sat next to his young charge. "What's wrong, Angela?"

"Nothing's wrong. I just don't want to do this anymore. It's my body and I wanna keep it the way it is."

Pastor Thoms tried a different tactic with her. "Pardon me, miss. But I don't believe I recognize you. My name is Pastor Thoms." He stuck out his hand for a shake.

Angela glared at him. "Are you tryin' to be funny?"

"Not at all. I'm trying to determine what's wrong. Look around you Angela… it's just us. Let your guard down, huh?"

Continuing to glare, she looked at Pastor Thoms. Then at Mrs. Thoms. And finally at her husband. That's when she melted. She slumped in her chair and immediately tears started flowing. "I don't understand why this is happening to me!" she bawled.

Pastor Thoms embraced her. "Why what's happening to you, dear?"

Collecting herself Angela inferred, "Everything bad always happens to me."

"Not everything," the pastor tried to encourage. "You have an amazing testimony, a beautiful family. And you've just married a wonderful man!"

Mrs. Thoms silently prayed. Raymond silently thanked God for the accolade.

Angela wasn't finished. "But I've been good… or at least I've tried to be. I ain't livin' that lifestyle anymore. Jesus told me He doesn't condemn me. So… why now? After livin' the way I'm supposed to and gettin' God's direction, why would He do this to me?"

Now Pastor Thoms understood. He gently pressed on Angela's shoulders to position her so she could look in his eyes. "Please understand something, my dear. Before we come to Christ, we live in sin and sow seeds to the flesh… seeds which produce bad fruit. Fruit of death, division, poor health. Those seeds don't grow into fruit overnight any more than you can plant a seed in the ground today and eat corn on the cob for dinner tomorrow." Angela half-smirked at this.

"So it is with our new life. While we now sow good seeds and wait for the proper time to reap a harvest, unfortunately we are still reaping the harvest from all the bad seeds we sowed. And some of us sowed a *lot* of bad seed. Even today I reap fruit from seeds I'd totally forgotten about years ago. Do you understand?"

"Yes," she confessed, "but I still don't feel any better."

Pastor Thoms embraced her again. "That's ok, dear. Just continue to trust that God knows what He's doing and will work everything out to the good."

"I'll try."

And with that, her name was called, and Ray escorted her to the room where nurses would converge on her body like it was a piece of meat and invade, molest and violate her entire person leaving nothing sacred. At least… it felt that way to Angela.

"Oh, Abba Father. I don't know what that was all about. I only know that I can trust You. Therefore, just as Jesus saw the faith of the friends of the paralytic so allow my trust to cover Angela's lack. She wishes she didn't have to go through this. I wish she didn't have to go through this! But help her to see this is for her own good and she will learn some valuable, cherish-able lessons about how much You love her as well as how You love her. And if you need to use me to help her see this, I'm Your vessel. I love You, in Jesus' name. Amen."

"Mr. Miller?" called the nurse as she glanced around the waiting room.

Ray arose from the little huddle in the corner composed of the Thoms, himself, and Ruby and Cole who arrived after school was let out. "Here!" he returned as his companions all glanced toward the nurse.

"Follow me, please," she instructed, turned and walked out the door.

He hurried to catch up. "Anything wrong?"

"No. Mrs. Miller is waking up. We told her we would come and get you."

'Mrs. Miller,' thought Ray to himself, considering how that probably would have a nice ring to it in other circumstances. The nurse showed him the recovery room and he tiptoed in as if his footsteps would create a tremor which may magnify Angela's discomfort. He stepped up to her bed, gazed upon her peaceful sleeping form, and gently touched her hand.

A look of pain crept across her face. "Don't touch me," she croaked without opening her eyes.

He jerked his hand back. "Oh, sorry," he whispered. "How do you feel?"

"How do you think I feel?" Ray just swallowed hard.

"This is all *your* fault," she managed with a little more force than she could physically handle, which caused her to groan. By *'your'* she didn't mean Ray. She meant *'your'* as in 'man'… not mankind in general, but 'man' as in the male gender.

"I don't understand," confessed Ray, confused.

"Ugh…" she groaned again, "I don't expect you to."

"Do you want me to go?" asked Ray, feeling rejected.

"Yes!" another groan due to careless physical exertion. Then she retracted, "No," much softer. There was a long pause as though she had fallen back to sleep. Finally, "Please stay… just don't say anything… and don't touch me." Ray obeyed.

He stayed by her side while she fell back to sleep. He watched as the staff tried to rouse her, to adjust her position. He held the pan as she vomited the nothing in her stomach. He observed as the nurses addressed all the discomfort and tearing this created in her body… adjusting, administering medication, utterly forcing her insides to cease rebelling against what had taken place. When Angela and her insides had finally calmed down, he followed the team to a semi-private room where she would spend the remainder of her stay. The other bed was empty, so the hospital offered it to Ray. He slept fitfully. He literally had no clue what was going on with his wife no matter how he had tried to be empathetic.

Ray finally dozed off around sunrise, but activity startled him back on full alert. An orderly brought Angela breakfast. A nurse raised her bed up so she could try to eat something and explained the doctor would be making his rounds soon.

Angela asked, "Why does my head hurt so bad – I don't even want to open my eyes?"

The nurse replied, "Probably from the anesthesia. The one we gave you might have been stronger than your body could handle. You gave us quite a scare yesterday. Maybe it would have been better to use a milder one... But you probably don't want to hear all this. I'll see if I can get something for your pain."

"Thanks," Angela offered and squinted. She glimpsed something out of the corner of her eye. Turning her head she opened one eye momentarily. "Ray?" You're still here?" she asked as though relieved from a heavy burden.

"Never left. Are you ok?" he sounded worried.

"I don't know. I hurt so bad. I don't know how they expect me to eat this stuff."

At that moment Ruby walked in. She had dropped off Cole at school and came right over.

As soon as Angela saw her she opened her arms. "Oh, Momma," she cried. While they embraced

Angela bawled… for a long time… until the nurse came in with some pain medication.

"Ok Lord, now I'm really scared. I mean Angela isn't being herself. Or maybe it's more like she's being her old self. I tried to encourage her by subtly suggesting I can't wait to see what she learns from this experience. And she said, 'You let them cut you in half and sew you back together and see how in the mood you are to learn something!' Of course maybe it has to do with her body being messed up. The doctor said she's still bleeding, and they need to get it to stop. God, please get her body back to acting right! I don't know what else to pray for besides that. I trust You, Lord. And somehow I believe deep down inside Angela trusts You. So I guess I'll leave it at that. Do what You do best… be God. I love You. Amen."

Later that day the Thoms came to see Angela one last time before leaving for Alabama. She beamed when they walked in.

Mrs. Thoms greeted her with a kiss. "How are you feeling?" "I never knew what terrible felt like until now." Mrs. Thoms laughed, which is what Angela intended.

Pastor Thoms asked, "Where's Ray?"

"Ugh. I sent him home… he's bein' too cheerful. But at the same time he's a nervous wreck. I don't think he got much sleep last night – he was here the whole time."

"It's difficult for him to comprehend what you're going through," offered Mrs. Thoms.

"And I realize that," agreed Angela. "But I don't have the strength right now to mentally support both of us. I'm on an emotional roller coaster. One minute I'm angry at myself for the choices I made which put me in this situation. The next, I'm gushin' love for my Momma, my baby, my new husband. Then, I'll be cryin' for no reason!"

"I know what you mean. It'll all subside eventually."

"And I believe you. I just wish it would hurry up. I hate it. I know its gonna take some time for things to get back to normal. I gotta be patient and not push too hard. And Ray's gotta be patient, too."

"There's no normal to get back to," Mrs. Thoms cautioned.

"What do you mean?" asked Angela.

"You are different now," she explained. "Your body had a major piece taken out of it yesterday."

Pastor Thoms added, "Plus, you are a newlywed. You are a couple now. And don't forget you're still a young Christian. If anybody has a reason to not look back, it's you."

Angela sighed suddenly feeling very tired. "You're right. Jesus told me, 'Go and sin no more.' And I've been *going* ever since."

"You've let God lead you into some strange and unfamiliar territory," reminded Mrs. Thoms.

"But He never left you," concluded her husband.

"And He won't leave me. I already know that. I just need to believe that, even when I forget it. Did that make sense? I'm feelin' really out of it."

"It made perfect sense. And we'll let you get some rest."

They kissed, embraced, promised to keep in touch. And Angela immediately fell asleep.

Then later that evening with her little family gathered around her they discussed dreams, plans, goals and no more looking back.

The next day when Ray arrived with a small bouquet of flowers he realized his token of affection would soon be lost in a veritable sea of love. There were cards, flowers, gifts, and people everywhere. Angela was glowing. She saw Ray and held up a little white teddy bear dressed as an angel that Brother Barclay had given her. Someone handed him an envelope containing donations to help with the hospital expenses. Ray set down his flowers, stepped back out into the hallway and wept.

From that moment he knew everything was going to be alright. He knew God had come through because his family – his church family – had come through. And they would become Angela's family as well. She would be attending church now with Ray not so that he could be her pastor, but because he was her companion. Ruby would attend regularly because she wanted to support her three favorite people in the world. And Cole would grow up learning who his *real* Father is.

"Dear Lord. Thank You for showing me I'm the one who needed to learn a lesson. And that I didn't have anything to worry about in regard to my relationship with You. Angela hasn't supplanted it – she expanded it! But I learned that I don't have the definitive answers on how You love us. The way You treat me is not the way You treat others, because we all have different relationships with You. Please forgive me for my pious prayer from before and for treating people like I have some kind of exclusive love connection with You. Help me to let You love me the way You see fit. Help me to let You love Angela the way You see fit. And help me to let You love anyone else the way You see fit. I love You, Lord. Amen."